King Arthur's Cave

First published: May 2005

ISBN: 0-86381-983-4

Cover design: Design Department of the Welsh Books Council

Published with the financial support of the
Welsh Books Council

Printed in Italy

Published by
Gwasg Carreg Gwalch, 12 Iard yr Orsaf, Llanrwst, Wales LL26 0EH
☎ 01492 642031   🖷 01492 641502
✆ books@carreg-gwalch.co.uk
Internet: www.carreg-gwalch.co.uk

Tales from Wales
2

King Arthur's Cave

Myrddin ap Dafydd
Translated by Siân Lewis
Illustrated by Robin Lawrie

The Aran is one of the finest mountains in Meirionnydd. It rises majestically above Bala Lake. Inside this mountain, so the story goes, a great Welsh hero has been sleeping for hundreds of years.

Dafydd was a shepherd boy who lived on a lonely farm on the slopes of the Aran. In the early spring, it was his job to take the sheep to the high pastures and make sure they stayed there to graze the fresh grass.

The sheep were stubborn, determined creatures. They knew the grass was sweeter on the lower slopes and they kept on running off down the mountain. The grass on the lower slopes was intended as winter feed for the cattle, so Dafydd had to chase after the sheep and drive them back up the Aran. It was very hard work being a shepherd.

"Breakfast's ready, Dafydd!" called his mother one morning.

Dafydd could hardly drag himself out of bed that morning. He didn't feel like chasing after the sheep all day.

To cheer him up, his mother said, "Come on now. You know what they say – tomorrow's only a day away. And it's the fair tomorrow, so you won't be working at all. You'll be off to Bala instead."

Bala Fair! Dafydd felt better as soon as he remembered the fair. He pictured the brightly-coloured stalls, the wonderful things for sale, the happy crowds and noisy showmen. Bala Fair was the best place in the world. Next day he'd be up first thing to walk the six miles to Bala to meet his friends with a spring in his step.

That morning, however, he had to walk along the sheep paths as usual.

By midday Dafydd and his dogs had rounded up the flock of sheep and driven them to a high valley that lay in the shadow of the mountain peak. He sat down under a hazel hedge to eat his lunch of bread and cheese. The dogs gathered round him and eyed the crusts hungrily.

When Dafydd next looked up, he saw that some of his sheep were already half way down the mountain. He lost his temper.

"Oh, botheration! Nel! Mot! Go and fetch them!" he shouted angrily.

The dogs were in no great hurry to move. Dafydd grabbed a stout straight piece of hazel growing from the base of the tree and leaned on it with all his weight. With a snap it broke off at the root. Whirling the branch round his head Dafydd ran after the straying sheep.

Dafydd was glad when his day's work was done. That evening he whittled away at his piece of hazel wood and shaped the scraggy branch into a neat shepherd's crook.

Next morning, at the crack of dawn, Dafydd set off for Bala Lake with his new crook in his hand. He reached Bala long before many of his friends had even got out of bed.

He wandered along the streets. It was fun watching the travelling merchants setting up their stalls. Some of them were quite strange-looking characters – the old man who was sitting on the large stone at the entrance to the inn, for instance . . .

Dafydd watched some farmers ride up on horseback. At the far end of the street a great brown bear was dancing to the sound of a fiddle. And there was the old man still sitting at the entrance to the inn . . .

For a split second he met the old man's eyes. A strange light burned in them. Dafydd turned away and walked down a back lane. When he glanced over his shoulder, he saw that the old man had got up and was following him.

In the back lane Dafydd turned sharp right, then left, and headed towards a crowd that had gathered around a gypsy caravan in front of the forge. All of a sudden a bony hand gripped his shoulder and forced him to stop.

Even before he turned, he knew whose hand it was. The old man who stood behind him had a grey flowing beard and a blue cloak that swirled around his tall, thin body.

"Who gave you that stick?" he demanded.

"I got it and carved it myself," replied Dafydd.

"Oh? And where did you get it from?" The old man's voice whispered, like the wind through a keyhole.

"On the slopes of the Aran . . . " Dafydd began.

"Come along and show me where," the man said. His bony hand gripped Dafydd's upper arm and began to steer him out of town.

"But I'm going to the fair," protested Dafydd. "I'm meeting my friends."

"No you're not, my boy. Not today." When Dafydd saw the fire in the old man's eyes, he knew it was no use arguing. "There'll be plenty more fairs in Bala," said the old man.

Soon the two of them were striding along the shores of the lake. The old man made sure they kept well away from the road where crowds of local people were heading towards the fair.

As soon as they reached the mountain path, the stranger in the blue cloak let go of Dafydd's arm.

"Can you remember exactly where you found your hazel stick?" he asked Dafydd.

"Yes. I'm up the mountain every day. It grew in a valley that I know very well."

"Then take me there, boy."

An hour later the two of them were standing in front of the hedge.

"That's the hole where I broke off the piece of wood," said the boy, pointing at the very spot.

"At last! The hole that leads to the treasure!" gloated the old man.

"What did you say?" asked Dafydd, staring at him in astonishment.

"This hole leads to a flight of steps, the steps lead down to the mouth of a cave and that cave is full of treasure. Enough gold and silver to fill all the stalls of Bala Fair."

"How do you know?" asked Dafydd.

"Because I'm a wizard," the old man answered. "A wizard knows everything about the stars, the earth and all that lies within. I saw the treasure in your stick this morning."

"A wizard!" exclaimed Dafydd.

The wizard took the stick from Dafydd's hand and pushed it into the hole that had been left when Dafydd had broken it the day before. Again and again he pulled it out and pushed it in, each time pressing deeper. At length they heard the stick strike a hard object underground.

The wizard knelt down and dug out the turf with his fingers. To Dafydd's surprise a large slab of slate appeared. With the end of the stick the wizard lifted a corner of the slab and pushed it to one side.

Dafydd peered into the dark space and saw steps leading down deep down into the heart of the mountain.

The wizard was rubbing his hands with glee and was dancing around on the spot like . . . like a little boy at the fair, thought Dafydd.

"Are you afraid to come down to the cave with me?" the old man challenged him.

"Not at all," replied Dafydd as bravely as he could.

Down they went into the blackness, down and down and down . . .

Dafydd could feel the steps beneath his feet. He slid his fingers along the damp tunnel walls. Soon the hole that had been opened under the hedge had shrunk to a distant pinpoint of light. By now the ground had flattened and Dafydd realised that the wizard had come to a halt in front of him.

"We're at the mouth of the cave," the wizard whispered. "Now, you must remember two things." His voice grew serious and his fingers felt along the tunnel walls as if he were searching for something. "First of all, you must keep your voice very quiet and . . . Ah! Here it is."

Through the gloom Dafydd made out the shape of an old lamp that the wizard had found hanging on the wall. The old man fumbled inside his cloak and soon there was a bright flash as he lit the lamp. Light flooded the tunnel.

"And the second thing," the wizard whispered, "if you value your life, do not touch that bell."

"This one?' asked Dafydd, pointing at an enormous bronze bell that hung overhead.

"Don't! DO NOT touch it! Duck down and follow me into the cave."

Dafydd crouched down and crept under the bell. When he lifted his head again, he saw a sight that took his breath away.

Heap upon heap of treasure sparkled in the lamplight, and made the cave as bright as day. There were chests full of gold and silver . . . shining shields studded with precious gems . . . ornate cups and dishes . . . solid Celtic crosses made of precious metals . . . fine armour . . .

Armour? Yes, there were dozens of swords . . .

And spears . . .

And arrows . . .

And . . . Good gracious! Soldiers!

Dafydd looked around him in a panic. In the cave in the heart of the mountain lay dozens of soldiers, each one with his weapons beside him. From the way their chests gently rose and fell, Dafydd realised they weren't dead, but fast asleep. That was a relief! They were all dressed in patterned woollen cloth and leather jerkins and some had wolf skins thrown over them. They wore Celtic chains and ornaments. Dafydd was amazed at their size and their strength. Their arms were like tree trunks. These were bold, mighty warriors, as hard as steel. They must be the finest soldiers who had ever walked this land, he thought.

At the far end of the cave, on a large old-fashioned chair, sat a man who was a little older than the rest. He wore silver armour, and carved on the back of his chair were ferocious red dragons. He slept with his head resting against his hands, and those hands held the hilt of the finest sword Dafydd had ever seen. He could not tear his eyes away from the long shining blade and the fiery hilt.

"Come on," whispered the wizard impatiently. "There's no time to lose. Fill up this sack so we can get out of here."

Dafydd turned round and saw the wizard kneeling amongst the treasure. He had several sacks hidden under his cloak and he was busy stuffing one of them full of gold and silver.

"But we can't . . . Whose treasure is it?" Dafydd asked, his voice sharp with fear. "Who . . . who are these soldiers and who's that man on the great throne?"

"Sh! It's King Arthur and the men sleeping around him are his finest soldiers. Now take this sack . . . "

"King Arthur? Wales's greatest hero! But I thought he had died hundreds of years ago after he beat the Saxons . . . "

"No, he's not dead. He's sleeping. The king brought his soldiers to this cave in the middle of the mountains and here he'll sleep till Wales and its people are ready for him."

"When will that be?" asked Dafydd.

"He has promised to return to lead his people when the children of Wales are true to their country. When that happens, someone will come to this cave, ring the bell and wake all the sleepers. Right, we've wasted enough time. Take this sack . . ."

The wizard had begun to fill a second sack as fast as he could. But Dafydd was shaking with fear.

"No, I can't," he said.

"Of course you can. Now where's the crown? Ah, there it is." The wizard made his way towards a small table beside the sleeping king. On the table sparkled a golden crown.

"That's Arthur's crown!" cried Dafydd, backing away. "Stop! You can't steal the king's crown!"

"This crown belonged to the greatest king Wales has ever seen," said the wizard with a smile. "Then for seven hundred years before it disappeared, it belonged to the kings and the princes of Wales. Now it belongs to me! To me!"

"No! No!" cried Dafydd as he stumbled backwards after the wizard towards the entrance of the cave.

Quickly the wizard turned round to warn him.

"Watch out for the . . . " but he was too late. Dafydd had stepped back too far and brushed against the bell. A long, clear note rang through the cave.

Dafydd grabbed the clapper to stop it sounding again, but the soldiers were already awake. They jumped to their feet and reached for their weapons, wielding their swords.

"Wake up. Wake up. It's day," they called to each other.

From the great throne a commanding voice spoke: "And who says it is day?"

The soldiers fell silent. They looked around and saw the wizard. He had dropped his sacks and stood near the bell with the shepherd boy beside him.

"Um . . . it was a mistake, your Majesty," the wizard said, bowing low. "This boy and I were looking for a lost sheepdog, when we happened to stumble across the entrance to the cave . . . "

"So the hour has not come," said King Arthur. "Seal the entrance after you. We have been called too soon, my soldiers. Wales is not yet ready. Go back to sleep."

Silently Dafydd and the wizard retreated up the stairs, leaving every single piece of treasure behind them.

A thin mist lay over the Aran mountain. Dafydd stepped out into the daylight and sat down once more under the hedge. He watched the wizard follow him from the tunnel, his face drawn and pale. The old man reached down and pushed the slate back over the hole that led to the cave.

A raven croaked overhead. Dafydd looked up, but the bird was lost in the mist.

When he looked back towards the tunnel entrance, the wizard had also disappeared. The ground before him lay unmarked. The shepherd got to his feet, picked up his sheep crook and hurried off down the mountain with his heart beating fast.

Afterwards, Dafydd returned many times to the slopes of the Aran to search for that valley. He never found it, nor did he find the hazel tree. He never again set eyes on the bearded wizard. But he kept that hazel crook till the end of his life. He also kept a flame of hope alive in his heart, for he knew that King Arthur would return one day to save his country – when Wales was ready for him.

Tales from Wales 1
Fairy Tales from Wales

There are many stories about the 'little people' of Wales – here are four of them.

Tales from Wales 3
The Faithful Dog, Gelert

The haunting story of Prince Llywelyn's favourite dog, the baby in the cradle and the wolf . . .

Tales from Wales 4
Black Bart, the Welsh Pirate

Did you know that the most successful and colourful pirate ever was a Welshman . . . ?